3/12

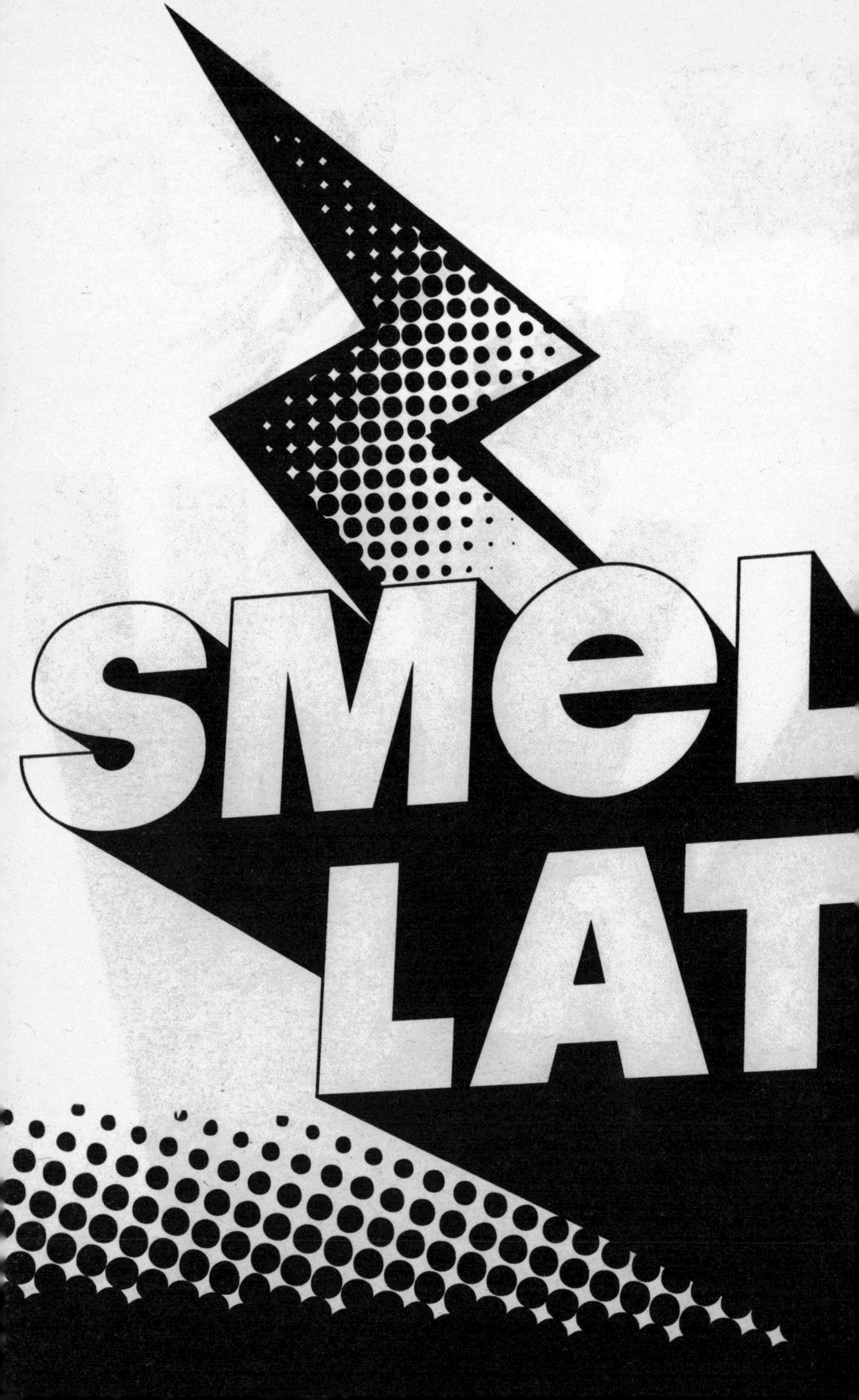
SMEL
LAT

YOU
ER!

adapted by **Kama Einhorn**

based on the screenplays **"Fanboy Stinks"**

and **"Night Morning"** by **Eric Horsted**

illustrated by **Steve Lambe**

Simon Spotlight/Nickelodeon

New York London Toronto Sydney New Delhi

designed by Victor Joseph Ochoa

Based on the TV series *Fanboy and Chum Chum*™ as seen on Nickelodeon™

SIMON SPOTLIGHT/NICKELODEON
An imprint of Simon & Schuster Children's Publishing Division 1230 Avenue of the Americas, New York, NY 10020. Copyright © 2012 Viacom International, Inc. All rights reserved. NICKELODEON, *Fanboy and Chum Chum,* and all related titles, logos, and characters are trademarks of Viacom International, Inc. All rights reserved, including the right of reproduction in whole or in part in any form. SIMON SPOTLIGHT and colophon are registered trademarks of Simon & Schuster, Inc. For information about special discounts for bulk purchases, please contact Simon & Schuster Special Sales at 1-866-506-1949 or business@simonandschuster.com.
Manufactured in the USA 0112 OFF
First Edition 10 9 8 7 6 5 4 3 2 1
ISBN 978-1-4424-2834-8 (pbk)
ISBN 978-1-4424-4685-4 (hc)
Library of Congress Control Number 2011944288

FANBOY
STINKS

What did one eye say to the other eye?

Between you and me, something smells.

CHAPTER ONE

Chum Chum leaned into the fridge, his butt sticking way up in the air, and tossed stuff out while madly sniffing around.

"No, that's not it," he said, cheerfully fighting the urge to throw up.

"Oh, horrible stench, where are you?" he sang out. He was totally puzzled. *Where could that disgusting odor be coming from?* "Hmm, maybe it's this cottage cheese." He took a whiff and immediately made a face.

"Smells like the cheese *died* in that cottage," he muttered.

Just then Fanboy walked by. He was in a great mood. "Whatcha doin', my pocket-size amigo?" he asked Chum Chum.

"Some horrible smell woke me up this morning," Chum Chum complained, "and I'm trying to figure out where it's coming from."

Fanboy smiled as flies buzzed around his dirt-streaked face. "A horrible smell, you say?" he asked, puffing up his chest. He stretched out his arms and legs proudly. "Is *this* the reek you seek?" he asked.

Plumes of stinky green fumes wafted from his body.

Chum Chum couldn't believe that his best friend was the source of the horrible stench! "Ugh! You smell like a foot and a Brussels sprout had a baby . . . who pooped in its diaper!"

Chum Chum's eyes watered; they were stinging from Fanboy's noxious odor.

"And how!" Fanboy said triumphantly. "You see, Chum Chum, modern man has forgotten what the caveman once knew. Stink *GOOOOD*!" He posed heroically as more fumes floated from his body. The flies buzzed about him happily.

Mortified, Chum Chum grabbed a hose and tried desperately to wash the stink off Fanboy. But Fanboy acrobatically wriggled and dodged and moved his body every which way to avoid getting wet. "No! Water no touchy! No washy!" he

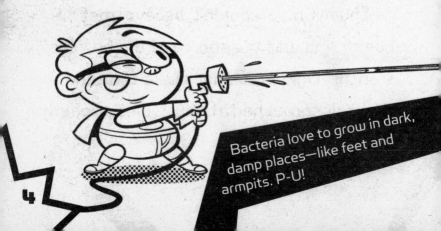

Bacteria love to grow in dark, damp places—like feet and armpits. P-U!

cried. "I'm shooting for the world record—longest time without taking a bath!"

Chum Chum turned off the water. A best friend had to be loyal, no matter what. "Okay, Fanboy. But if it's all right with you, I'm gonna keep my face in this." He stuck his nose back into the tub of rancid cottage cheese.

"Oh, yeah, that's better," he said with a contented sigh.

What did the judge say when the skunk showed up?

"Odor in the court!"

CHAPTER TWO

The next day, a crowd of flies and seagulls circled in the air as Fanboy and Chum Chum sat in the school cafeteria. "What is it with those gulls?" Fanboy wondered.

"Well, you smell like a dead crab," Chum Chum reminded him.

Fanboy took a deep breath. "With a hint of butt," he added, his smile practically bigger than his whole dirty face.

At that moment Chum Chum noticed two bumps that had started growing from Fanboy's gloved right hand. "Hey, what are those?" he asked nervously, pointing to the bumps.

Fanboy took a closer look. "I'm growing mushrooms!" he exclaimed. He almost sounded a little disappointed in his dirtiness. Almost. The next second later, he beamed and proudly declared, "I am dis-GUST-ing! Whoo!"

Chum Chum couldn't take it anymore. His best friend smelled *terrible*. He could only think of one way to escape the reek.

What do you call a witch's chant that causes a terrible odor?

The smell spell.

Chum Chum reached up and removed his own nose! But the persistent green fumes found another opening.

"It's no use," Chum Chum groaned as he ran out of the cafeteria. "I can still smell you through my ears!"

Fanboy shrugged. "Okay, smell ya later!" he called out, cheerfully basking in his own disgustingness.

"Not if I smell you first," Chum Chum

replied ruefully. Then he turned to barf in a hallway trash can, much to Janitor Poopatine's dismay.

Fanboy turned his attention to his lunch. "Time for some liverwurst," he said, before taking a nibble. "A food that smells almost as bad as me!"

Suddenly Fanboy heard a voice. "Pssst," it whispered. He looked around, but couldn't see anyone. He heard the voice again: "Pssst." It was definitely coming from nearby. *Very* nearby. And then he heard, "Hey, pally, you wanna break me off a piece of that wurst? Clothes gotta eat, too, you know. C'mon!"

Fanboy's eyes widened as he stared at the glove on his own right hand. The mushroom bumps had grown into two eyes with bushy eyebrows!

"Whoa!" Fanboy exclaimed. "Suit, you're *alive*! But how?"

His gloved hand answered him right back. "You know that old saying, 'You don't wash that suit, it's gonna walk around by itself'? Well, that's me! Call me Stinks."

Fanboy was excited. It wasn't every day that clothes talked to him, and even better, it was his own stinky suit! "Wow! Nice to meet you, Stinks."

"Ol' Stinks is a little hungry, you know what I'm sayin'?" Stinks said. "You think that kid over there will share his sandwich with us?"

"Uh, I don't know," Fanboy said, feeling torn. He did want to please Stinks, but he didn't want any trouble. "Chris Chuggy always cleans his plate. Rumor has it that sometimes he even *eats* his plate."

Stinks pinched Fanboy's face affection-
ately. "Aw, you could convince him. C'mon,
kid! You got charm!"

Fanboy blushed and grinned. "I have to
say, Stinks, you are one flattering suit."

Encouraged, Fanboy walked up to
Chris Chuggy, who was gobbling his
sandwich. "Hey, Chris," Fanboy began. "My
suit and I were wondering if you'd share—"

But Chris wouldn't let him finish. With
one whiff of Fanboy and Stinks, Chris
started wailing, "Wah, wah, waaaah!"

Fanboy put his hands on his hips. He could tell Chris was going to be a big, selfish baby. Oh, well.

But on the other hand, literally, Stinks wasn't giving up so fast. He leaned in close to Chris's face. "Oh, don't wanna share, huh?" he snapped. Then he released a giant green stink spray. "How do ya like that?"

Chris started to gurgle, shudder, and moan. Then his eyes and ears popped

off of his head and he rolled out of the cafeteria to escape the foul smell.

"Wow!" Fanboy said, clearly impressed. He couldn't believe he had the good fortune of having a right hand that was so talented—and so stinky!

"What'd I tell ya, pal?" Stinks said. "Now let Ol' Stinks here have a taste." He took a big chomp of Chris's sandwich.

Fanboy was thrilled. What else could they get to eat? He looked around and spotted Lupe and her two friends. "Hey, they have pudding," he told Stinks. "I wonder if they'd like to share too."

"Let's find out," Stinks said enthusiastically.

"Hey, guys, have you met Stinks?" Fanboy asked the group as he walked over to them. Lupe's friends were so horrified by the stinky fumes that they all jumped into Lupe's open mouth. With that, Lupe flapped her arms, and flew into the air, away from the awful aroma. Fanboy shrugged and sat down with Stinks to eat.

After slurping up the pudding, Fanboy and Stinks decided to share their superb stinkiness with the school cheerleaders. "*Helloooo*, ladies!" Fanboy called to the girls as he grabbed one of their megaphones—and funneled his stink right into their noses.

"Give me an EEEW!" one of them said, gasping for breath.

"Two, four, six, eight, I think I might regurgitate!" said another, choking on her words.

"Let's GOOOOOOO AWAY!" They chanted as they piled up into a perfect cheerleading formation and disappeared from the scene.

Fanboy and Stinks feasted on the sandwiches and milk the cheerleaders left behind.

"Wow, Stinks!" Fanboy said, chewing happily with his mouth wide open. "This is incredible! It's like people see us in a whole new way." He paused before

adding, "Maybe it's because their eyes are watering."

Stinks chuckled. "Hey, we're just gettin' started!" He held up his milk carton to make a toast. "To the good life!"

Fanboy eagerly took a sip. "Eww, it's curdled."

"Yeah," Stinks admitted. "You get used to it."

People can recognize about 10,000 different odors. That is a lot! And the ones they can't recognize, they don't want to know about!

CHAPTER THREE

When he got to class, Fanboy stood in line to turn in his homework. That's when he realized he had left it back at the Fanlair. Luckily Stinks was on hand to help out. "Don't worry, I'll take care of it," Stinks said out of the corner of his mouth.

Soon Fanboy was at the front of the line. "Papers, please," bellowed Mr. Mufflin.

Stinks waved in front of the teacher's face. "You don't need to see our papers,"

Stinks said firmly, spewing green fumes.

Mr. Mufflin's eyeballs rolled around in his head. "I don't need to see your papers," he repeated in a robotic voice.

"You think you'll go grab forty winks in the teacher's lounge," Stinks continued.

"I think I'll go grab forty winks in the teacher's lounge," Mr. Mufflin echoed.

"Wearing this pretty hat!" Fanboy added, putting a wide-brimmed straw hat on his teacher.

"Wearing this pretty hat!" Mr. Mufflin repeated. With that, he walked away, happily.

Fanboy and Stinks high-fived each other.

"So what was that?" Fanboy asked Stinks. "Some sort of stink-eye mind trick?"

"Yeah, something like that," Stinks replied. "I call it 'The Fuhgeddaboutit!'"

When you don't wash, your sweat stays on your body, mixing with the bacteria on your skin to give it that delicious foul scent. Best thing to do is not wait for your clothes to come to life—wash up!

Some people get paid to smell stuff. Laboratories hire them when they are testing a new product like shampoo or deodorant. Too bad no one gets paid to be smelly!

Your sense of smell is weakest in the morning; your ability to smell gets better as the day goes on. So "morning breath" would actually smell worse if it happened at night!

CHAPTER FOUR

That afternoon Chum Chum walked by the bake sale table in the hallway and was shocked. "The charity bake sale's tonight?" he exclaimed. "I better get started on my pecan log!"

Nancy Pancy tried hard to not hurt Chum Chum's feelings. "Uh, Chum Chum," she said. "Maybe this year you shouldn't make your pecan log. We still haven't been able to get rid of last year's." She nodded over at Janitor Poopatine, who was struggling to remove a year-old pecan log from the floor.

But Chum Chum didn't get her point. "We just need a fresh pecan log. I'm on it!"

Chum Chum hurried off. Just then he saw Fanboy and Stinks striding down the hallway, acting as if they owned the place. An extremely strong odor oozed from them, knocking out everyone they passed.

"Hey, Chum Chum!" Fanboy called. "You'll never believe what happened to my suit!"

Chum Chum covered his nose. *How was it possible that Fanboy smelled even worse than he did at lunch?* "No time to smell! Pecan log!" Chum Chum yelled as he ran away.

Fanboy looked at Stinks. "Chum Chum doesn't know what he's missing, Stinks. I'm having the time of my life. And I'm learning so much!"

"Yeah, you done good, kid," Stinks said. "Now it's time we cook up a bake job!"

"A bank job?" Fanboy asked. *Uh-oh. Was he going to have to rob a bank?*

"No, not a bank job," said Stinks. "A *bake* job. See this bake sale? We're gonna rob it. We'll be up to our wrists in pastries! Heh, heh, heh."

"Rob?" Fanboy asked, raising his eyebrows. He started to get nervous. "Question: Is that like stealing? And a follow-up question: Isn't stealing wrong?"

"Ha, ha, ha," Stinks said, poking Fanboy in the eye. "You're funny, Flatsie. You amuse me. Like a clown."

"Y-yeah," Fanboy stammered. "You know what might be funnier than robbing the bake sale? If we just . . . fuhgeddaboutit?" He laughed weakly.

Stinks quickly shot back, "You turning squirrelly on me?"

"Me, squirrelly? Don't be silly," Fanboy said, as he busily gnawed on an acorn.

"You gonna come along with me on this or what?" Stinks demanded.

Did you know that no one smells the same odor in the same way? So a rose or a piece of blue cheese may smell nicer to some people than to others. Find something that smells really bad, and see if your friends think so too. Go ahead, they'll love this game!

Fanboy was afraid to disagree with Stinks. "Sure thing, Stinks," he said. "Heh, heh. I am your right-hand man. . . ."

"Okay then, listen up," Stinks said as he pointed to a drawing he'd posted inside Fanboy's locker. "Since you've never

done a bake job, I'll keep it simple. First we blanket the area in stink, clearing out any potential witnesses. Then we empty out the cupcake table. Then we move over to assorted breads and puffs. And on our way out, we hit the big-ticket item...hello, pecan log. Think you can handle that?"

Wait a second! THE PECAN LOG? The one Chum Chum was always so proud of? Fanboy couldn't do that to his best friend. Fanboy had to convince Stink that taking the pecan log was not a good idea.

"Well, actually—" he began.

"Good. I gotta go to the bathroom before we get started," Stinks replied.

Fanboy patiently waited outside the bathroom with his arm stretched out, his hand being attached and all. The whole time he tried to come up with ways to get out of the bake sale robbery.

Just then Chum Chum walked by, dragging his freshly made—and very heavy—pecan log. Fanboy had never been happier to see him. "Chum Chum!

I'm so glad you're here," he said. "Listen, I need your help. My suit came to life, and it's making me rob the bake sale!"

But Chum Chum didn't seem the least bit concerned. "GOOD NEWS!" he said loudly. "I put plugs in my nose *and* my ears so I can't smell you. Isn't that GREAT?"

Fanboy called after him, "Chum Chum! You don't understand. We gotta stop the suit."

But Chum Chum couldn't hear him.

Only Stinks heard Fanboy—and he was not pleased at all.

"Never figured you for a rat, kid," he told Fanboy.

"Me, a rat?" Fanboy replied. "Don't be silly." He nervously nibbled on a wedge of cheese.

"Let me clear out your ears so you really hear this," Stinks said sternly as he poked his finger in one ear, all the way through Fanboy's head, and out the other ear.

"Hey, that's not comfortable!" Fanboy yelled.

"Now you listen here, Flatsie, *I* call the shots," Stinks reminded him. "And anybody who doesn't like it gets whacked."

"Uh, whacked?"

Stinks whacked Fanboy in the face. "I'm a hand, I whack things. Now don't make me whack you again."

"Okay."

Stink patted Fanboy's cheek. "That's a good boy. Now let's go."

Why, why, why didn't I wash my suit? Fanboy wondered. *Then Stinks wouldn't have come to life and taken over mine!*

He swallowed hard and looked around. Everyone was happily munching on the goodies from the bake sale. More flies buzzed around him than ever before. Fanboy was miserable. On top of that, his throat was dry. He needed a drink at the water fountain.

Oh, wait, he reminded himself. *That's the crazy fountain that always sprays me.*

Suddenly Fanboy had an idea—a brilliant plan—one that was sure to solve his "Stinks" problem once and for all.

What do you call someone who insists on smelling everything?

Nosy.

1 in 1,000 people cannot smell butyl mercaptan, the stinky smell of skunks. Good for them. Bad for those of us who are among the 999 who can!

CHAPTER FIVE

My water fountain plan's so crazy, it just might work! Fanboy thought excitedly. Clean water would ruin Stinks. Of course, it would also rinse off Fanboy's stink. But that seemed a small price to pay to get out of this life of crime—*and* help Chum Chum sell his pecan log.

"Hey, snap out of it!" Stinks snarled. "It's almost showtime."

But Fanboy went up to the water

fountain and declared, "You're all washed-up, Stinks!" Fanboy pressed the button and waited for the water to start spraying, but the water fountain worked normally! What was going on?

"What? Where's the crazy spray?" Fanboy asked, exasperated.

"I think you'll find that the water fountain is fully operational," Janitor Poopatine said darkly as he passed by. He covered his nose at the smell of Fanboy as he added, "You're welcome."

"So," said Stinks, "you were tryin' to get me to go clean, huh? Of all the dirty tricks! Well, nobody tries to rinse Stinks out. We're robbing this joint whether you like it or not."

But Fanboy had had enough. He was no longer going to be the right-hand man to his own right hand! "Over my smelly body, Stinks!" They wrestled each other in an all-out battle to gain the upper hand. It was good versus evil, right versus wrong, right versus left, stinky versus stinker!

At that very moment, Chum Chum came along, dragging his beloved pecan log to the bake sale table. "It's really dense this year," he told Nancy Pancy proudly. He hoisted it up onto the table, but it was so heavy that the table broke. He whispered to Nancy Pancy, "I ran out of sand, so I used gravel instead."

"Uh, great, Chum Chum," Nancy said, not thankful at all. "Why don't you put it over there." She pointed to the other end of the table. Chum Chum dutifully dragged the log and once again lifted it onto the table. It was so heavy that it launched Lupe—who was standing on the other end of the table—into the air.

"Aiiiiyeeeee!" she yelled as she crashed back down onto the table. This sent the pecan log flying into the air, and sailing

over Fanboy and Stinks, who were still wrestling on the floor.

"Give it up," Stinks snapped.

All of a sudden the superheavy pecan log landed on top of the water fountain. The fountain smashed and water began to gush out of the wall—right into Stinks, knocking him flat and washing him clean!

What did the veterinarian say when someone brought her a sick skunk?

"Oh no! My beautiful dirt. It's gettin' rubbed out!" Stinks cried.

"Forgive me, Stinks," said Fanboy dramatically. "I didn't want it to end this way. It's just that . . . I wanted to *smell* bad . . . not to *be* bad."

Stinks was fading fast. "Hey, kid," he whispered weakly. "Fuh . . . fuh . . . fuhgeddaboutit."

"I'll never forget ya, Stinks," Fanboy said. He was more than ready to move on with normal life, but he was still a little sad his stink was gone.

Chum Chum sniffed Fanboy. He smelled . . . clean. "I guess this means no world record," Chum Chum said sympathetically.

"Sometimes this job really stinks."

"That's okay, Chum Chum. I have a backup," Fanboy said. "I'm going to set a record for most days without . . . brushing my *teeth*!" Green and brown fumes shot out of Fanboy's mouth and went right up Chum Chum's nose.

Chum Chum froze; his eyes were wide and his body rigid.

Fanboy grinned. "C'mon, buddy, I'll take you home."

As Fanboy happily walked home, a foul-smelling puddle of dirty water slid down the hall and surrounded Janitor Poopatine's shoes. Suddenly each shoe sprouted eyes and a mouth. They cackled evilly. Stinks was back!

Only this time he was Janitor Poopatine's very stinky problem.

THE END

**NIGHT
MORNING**

What time is it when you wake up in the middle of the night?

Time to go back to sleep.

CHAPTER ONE

"Sleep tight, buddy," Fanboy said as he tucked his best friend, Chum Chum, into bed for the night. Chum Chum snuggled under his covers.

Then he got out of bed so that he could tuck in Fanboy. They repeated this routine every night.

Chum Chum smiled. "And there *you* go. Good night. Sleep tight. Don't let the bed bugs bite."

"But they might!" Fanboy added, and they both cracked up. The two friends never got tired of their nightly routine. But Fanboy was tired. In less than a second, he was asleep and snoring.

After a few moments, however, something woke him up.

"Okay, Chum Chum. I'll retuck you," he muttered automatically. But when he looked over at Chum Chum's empty bed, he gasped. "Chum Chum! Where are you?"

Fanboy found Chum Chum coming up the steps.

"Fanboy!" said Chum Chum. "What are you doing up? That monster under your bed kicking you again?"

"No, we worked it out," Fanboy replied. The giant tentacles reached out from under Fanboy's bed and gave a friendly wave. "It's all good, bro," the monster agreed.

"Why are you awake, Chum Chum?" Fanboy asked.

"Oh, I was enjoying my Night Morning," Chum Chum replied.

"Night Morning? What's that?"

"Night Morning is the time between night and morning when you can do all the cool stuff you can't do between morning and night," Chum Chum explained patiently.

"Whoa, whoa, whoa," said Fanboy, picking Chum Chum up to stop him from walking away. "What kind of cool stuff?"

"Cool Night Morning stuff, silly."

"Wow," Fanboy said. This Night Morning thing sounded good. Chum Chum definitely had his attention. "Would you take a few follow-up questions?"

"Sure."

Fanboy fired off his questions a mile a minute. "Can you eat sweet potatoes? Can you play Chimp Chomp? Can you read comic books? Can you break-dance? Can you talk to fish? Can you eat cheese through your ear? Can you chew gum while walking? Are there rocket cars? Are they red? Are there blueberries? Are *they* red?"

Fanboy just could not stop asking about Night Morning. He asked Chum Chum questions all through the next day, at school, and then at home again. He didn't even stop when he was brushing his teeth.

"Can you wear clown shoes? Can you drink pudding through a straw? Can you ride a dog like a horse? Are the banks open? Can you dance with mummies?

Can you get a good bagel? Does it rain hot gravy? Will a Sasquatch give back rubs? Does it rain hot gravy? Are there unlimited chicken drummettes? Do monkeys shine your shoes?"

"Well—" Chum Chum began.

But Fanboy wasn't done. "Can you eat electricity? Can you pet a live tiger?"

When he finished his bathroom business, he added another important question: "Can you hand me some toilet paper?"

Then he went back to asking Chum Chum even more about Night Morning. "Can you wear white after Labor Day? Do the shrimp peel and eat themselves?

Of course they do! What am I thinking? It's Night Morning! Anything can happen!"

"I don't know if you're interested, but if you want, you can do Night Morning with me," Chum Chum offered as they were getting ready for bed.

Fanboy's eyes popped out of his head. "Me? Do Night Morning? I'm going to do Night Morning!"

Fanboy couldn't wait. He sang himself a lullaby and quickly fell asleep, dreaming of all the great things Night Morning would bring.

CHAPTER TWO

Chum Chum's alarm clock rang. "Night Morning. Night Morning. Night Morning. Night Morning," it announced.

Chum Chum yawned and stretched his little body. "Fanboy, it's time," he whispered.

But Fanboy hardly moved. "Muh," he said.

"It's Night Morning!" Chum Chum yelled into Fanboy's ear.

Fanboy awoke with a start. "Night

Morning!" he exclaimed. "I can't believe it's finally—"

Ding dong! Fanboy was interrupted by the sound of the doorbell.

"Who could that be?" Chum Chum wondered as Fanboy went to open the door.

"C'mon in, guys!" Fanboy greeted.

"Uhhh, what's happening?" Chum Chum asked.

"I invited everybody to spend Night Morning with us!" Fanboy said proudly as

a whole bunch of people, including Jack, Lupe, Mr. Mufflin, Francine, Kyle, Michael Johnson, Chris Chuggy, and Yo trooped in.

"I don't know, Fanboy, Night Morning may not be everyone's cup of tea . . . ," Chum Chum said, scratching his head. He wasn't sure he really wanted to share Night Morning with so many people.

"Chum Chum, ol' chum," Fanboy said, trying to sound wise. "You've discovered something wonderful. Something sacred."

Jack put a dollar in Fanboy's hand as he stepped into the room.

Chum Chum was shocked. "You're *charging* people?"

"Hey, if you wanna see something sacred, you gotta pony up the clams!" Fanboy said as he collected money from everyone.

"There *will* be clam ponies here, right, Chum Chum?" Without waiting for an answer, Fanboy announced, "We got clam ponies! Is everyone excited?"

"Yay!" the crowd cheered.

"Okay, everybody," Fanboy shrieked. "Hike up your pants 'cause there's gonna be a flood of awesomeness!"

"I've never been so excited," Lupe said unexcitedly.

Chum Chum isn't the only one who knows about Night Morning. So do owls, cats, bats, coyotes, opossums, and raccoons. That's because they're nocturnal. That means they are up at night and asleep during the day. Like Man-Arctica. How's that for science?

Knock-knock.

Who's there?

Hoo.

Hoo who?

Hoo hoo, I'm an owl. Want to do Night Morning with me?

CHAPTER THREE

hum Chum, let's get this party started!" Fanboy cried. The crowd cheered. "Okay, everybody, settle down," Fanboy said. He and Chum Chum led everyone into the kitchen, where Chum Chum stood on a stool in front of the fridge.

"Well, the tension is palpable. I think we all feel it. I know *I* do." Fanboy held a microphone in front of Chum Chum's face. "So I think what everybody wants to know is: How? Do? You? Get this

Night Morning started?"

"Well, um. I . . . I guess I usually start with . . . uh . . . a bowl of cereal?" Chum Chum replied.

"Did you hear that folks? He said CEREAL!" The crowd cheered and waved their hands high in the air.

"Okay, he's reaching for the cereal box," Fanboy said in his best sports announcer voice. The crowd cheered again. "We do not know what he's going to choose. But it is sure to be the most dangerously giant bowl of the sweetiest, stickiest, most teeth-rottingest cereal ever!"

Everyone watched closely. Even Mr. Mufflin gulped loudly.

"He's grabbing a box—ooh, it's the Ice Monster Crunch Crunch!" Fanboy announced. "Folks, *this* is what you came to see!"

Everyone was taking pictures.

"What's he gonna do with the cereal?" Fanboy asked the crowd. "The possibilities are endless!"

Chum Chum ate his cereal slowly and happily.

Lupe said, "He's just eating it."

"Yeah, even I can do that," said Mr. Mufflin.

"Yeah, that's because he's getting to the *big finish*," Fanboy explained.

The crowd gasped, then sighed loudly when Chum Chum ate the last bite. Francine especially had quite a scowl on her face. "Okay, you said this was going to be really exciting," she said. "And instead, *hello*, it's really boring."

But nothing could dampen Fanboy's enthusiasm. "That's the beauty of Night Morning—it's unpredictable!"

"I'm so out of here," she said, and stomped off.

"Whoa, I did not see that one coming," Fanboy said.

When does Man-Arctica get cold feet?

When he walks around brrrr-footed.

Knock-knock.

Who's there?

Night.

Night who?

'Night. Morning will be here soon!

CHAPTER FOUR

Next I usually watch my favorite show," Chum Chum continued as he sat on the couch in front of the television.

"You know, I think we all knew we were in for something special this Night Morning, but this . . . is even specialer," Fanboy reported as Chum Chum stared at the blank screen. "You want me to turn that on for you, buddy?"

"Shhh," Chum Chum said. "It *is* on."

He stared at the black screen. *"In my imagination!"*

"That boy is crazy, like my uncle," Lupe said. "He married a chicken. Oh, they *fiiiight.*"

"Come on, guys, don't you just *love* Night Morning?" There was no stopping Fanboy. "Just when you think you're gonna get THIS . . ."—he held up his hand as if measuring something very tall—"you get THIS!" He held his hand lower, as if measuring something much shorter.

"Then I'll be taking *this*!" Kyle said, grabbing his money out of Fanboy's hand.

"Huh?" Fanboy said. "Two dollars? You only paid a dollar!"

"Pain and suffering," Kyle said, and stomped off.

"I'd rather watch my aunt lay eggs," said Lupe, as she also took her money back and stomped off.

But nothing could dampen Fanboy's excitement. "Hey, it's their loss, you know," he said, "'cause it's just about to get wild! Isn't that right, Chum Chum?"

"Well, I do have a shirt to iron. . . ." Chum Chum said over the sound of Chris Chuggy snoring. Everyone sighed loudly as Chum Chum began ironing. More people left.

But Fanboy was not discouraged. "Man, can he fluff and fold or what?" he gushed.

Then Chum Chum sharpened pencils. Another group walked out.

"Sharper! Sharper! Sharper!" Fanboy cheered. "C'mon, everyone now. Sharper! Sharper!"

Then Chum Chum cleaned his ears out with cotton swabs.

"He's cleaning the right. Now the left!" Fanboy reported.

Then Chum Chum knitted.

"Knit one, purl one. Knit one, purl one. Can this kid make a scarf or what?" By now, there were only a couple of guests left.

"Hey, where you going?" Fanboy asked his departing friends. "Aww, forget it. More fun for us! 'Cause the best is yet to come! Right, Chris Chuggy? The Chugmeister."

"Wah wah. Whoa," said Chris.

"Okay, Chum Chum, what's next?" Fanboy asked.

"Well, I could shake the crumbs out of the toaster." Then Chum Chum shook his head. "Oh, what am I saying? This is the part of Night Morning when Man-Arctica, the subzero hero, flies in."

"Whaaa? Man-Arctica comes here?" Fanboy's eyes popped out.

"Yeah, but only to give me super-powers. Then I usually help him protect the universe. Time permitting."

"DID YOU HEAR THAT? MAN-ARRRRRC-TIIIII-CAAAAAAAA!" Fanboy

screamed, his entire body vibrating with joy. He shook Chris Chuggy with all his might.

"Wah wah wah wah wah!" Chris Chuggy whined.

"Ooh, Man-Arctica," Yo said.

"I'm gonna meet Man-Arctica!" Fanboy said as Chum Chum set out cookies and milk. "Oh man, oh man, do I love Night—" Fanboy suddenly stopped. "What are you doing?"

"Putting out cookies and milk," Chum Chum replied calmly.

"Wha?" Chris Chuggy asked.

"I'll tell you *wha*," Chum Chum said, a little defensively. "Man-Arctica gets very very hungry from flying around the world delivering toys to all the good little boys and girls."

"Isn't that Santa Claus?" Yo asked, her hands folded across her chest.

"Who?" wondered Chum Chum.

Chris Chuggy and Yo looked at each other and rolled their eyes. Clearly they had seen and heard enough.

What is the name of Man-Arctica's mother's sister?

Aunt-Arctica.

The moon rises when the sun is still out. Look closely and you can see the sun and the moon at the same time of day. It's kind of like Night Morning. Only without a subzero hero.

What do you get when you cross Man-Arctica with a vampire?

Frostbite.

CHAPTER FIVE

ey, where you guys going? Man-Arctica's gonna be here any minute!" Fanboy said. But it was too late. He and Chum Chum were now alone.

"Yeah, I have a feeling this might be the night he finally comes," Chum Chum said with a grin.

Fanboy froze. "You mean he's never come before?"

"Nope! This'll be his first time ever."

Fanboy was silent for a moment. "So that means that I'm here for Man-Arctica's debut appearance! I mean, it just keeps getting more exciting!"

"So you wanna wait up for Man-Arctica with me?" Chum Chum asked.

"Do I? I wouldn't miss it," Fanboy said. "Now, let me just get my own comfy chair so I don't miss a single—"

Fanboy had fallen asleep before he even finished talking. But Chum Chum barely noticed that Fanboy had conked out. He was too busy remembering

something very important.

"Wait a minute! It's not cookies and milk. It's *milk and cookies*!" He quickly rearranged them. "There. Somehow that just feels more right."

And then, there he was, in the Fanlair's doorway. Man-Arctica. He was huge and blue and gray and wearing his gleaming ice suit. He was AMAZING.

"Man-Arctica! You came!" Chum Chum cried.

Man-Arctica seemed very happy to see the milk and cookies. "If there's one thing I love more than a snow cone on the frozen tundra, it's milk and cookies!" Man-Arctica said. "But *not* cookies and milk. I got so sick on that one time."

"Fanboy! Fanboy! Man-Arctica's here for Night Morning!" Chum Chum said to his sleeping buddy.

"Too tired," Fanboy murmured. "Worn out. Night Morning too intense. Go without me."

"You sure?"

Fanboy snored as Man-Arctica chugged his milk and ate his cookies. His hand was so big it almost couldn't hold the tiny cup, but he managed.

"Ahhh," he said when he had finished his snack. "So junior hero, shall we solve problems involving heat together?"

"You bet! Hey, can we take Fanboy?"

"Is he cool?" Man-Arctica asked. Chum Chum nodded. For sure, Fanboy was cool.

"All right. LET'S BREAK ARCTIC WIND!" Man-Arctica picked up Chum Chum, who picked up Fanboy, and they flew into the sky.

"Wheee!" said Chum Chum, as they rose in a dazzling, whirling tornado.

"Hey, if you don't mind, on the way, I gotta deliver a lot of presents to good boys and girls," Man-Arctica said once they were at a high cruising altitude.

"Sure, no problem," Chum Chum said. "Hey, have you heard of this Santa Claus guy?"

"Who?" Man-Arctica said.

"That's what I said!" Chum Chum said with a laugh. "Boy, Fanboy's really gonna love this when he wakes up!"

THE eND